LOVE AT LAST

MARKED BY HIS ALPHA

SOPHIE O'DARE

LOVE AT LAST

Copyright © 2024 by Sophie O'Dare

All rights reserved. No part of this publication may be reproduced, distributed, or transmitted in any form or by any means, including photocopying, recording, or other electronic or mechanical methods, without the prior written permission of the writer, except in the case of brief quotations embodied in critical reviews and certain other noncommercial uses permitted by copyright law.

This is a work of fiction. Names, characters, businesses, places, events and incidents are either the products of the author's imagination or used in a fictitious manner. Any resemblance to actual persons, living or dead, or actual events is purely coincidental.

Cover Design Copyright © 2023 Lyn Forester

Printed in the United States of America.

First Printing, 2024

ALSO BY SOPHIE O'DARE

HIS ALPHA UNIVERSE

Marked by His Alpha

Bad With Love

Maybe Tomorrow

Omega on the Run

Desperate to Marry

Leading Love

Focused on Him

Taking Two

Faking for Real

Taming His Alpha

Love at Last

Taken by His Alpha

Claimed by the Boss

~

Tails x Horns

You to Me

Just Not You

As You Are

Kiss Me Please *(novella)*

Heat Me Up *(novella)*

Play With Me

~

Sweet Blood

First Bite

For future Sophie O'Dare releases, keep an eye on:

www.SophieODare.com

LOVE AT LAST
Marked by His Alpha Book 10

Can the magic of a wedding heal a broken heart?

When Brad sets off to attend the wedding of his foster mom, the last person he expects to see there is his first love, the Alpha whose heart he broke.

Against the backdrop of a summer night, with music in the air and love on the line, can Brad win back the only man he's ever wanted, or will the mistake of his youth leave him alone on the dance floor?

About Alpha/Beta/Omega in this Universe

Alpha: Can be male or female. Naturally charismatic with a dominant personality, so they tend to be in positions of power. Can use Command to enforce their will on weaker Alphas and Omegas who are not protected by an Alpha. When near an Omega in Heat, Alpha's are driven to protect and mate with the Omega.

Beta: Can be male or female. Regular citizens without any atypical behavioral traits. Are not affected by an Alpha's Command or an Omega's Heat.

Omega: Can be male or female, and both genders are capable of becoming pregnant during their Heat. Omegas, up until recently, have struggled to hold onto regular jobs due to going into Heat every month. During Heat, they release a pheromone that attracts Alphas. The pheromone can now be suppressed through the use of suppressants.

Nape Guard: A band around the neck with a protective plate at the back the covers an Omega's nape and protects them from being Marked against their will.

Suppressants: Medication Omegas take to help suppress their pheromones during their monthly Heat.

Heat: A three day period every month in which Omegas release a pheromone to attract an Alpha and are overwhelmed with the need to mate. The effects can be reduced by the use of suppressants.

Command: An Alpha's ability to enforce their will on weaker Alphas and on Omegas. Betas are not affected by an Alpha's command.

Mark: During Heat, an Alpha is driven to Mark their partner by biting the back of their neck. The Mark stays in place for a month, claiming the breeding right of the Marked Omega. It also stops other Alphas from Commanding the Marked Omega. If the same Alpha Marks an Omega three times, it becomes permanent. If the Alpha does not

Lore

Mark the Omega, the Mark fades after their next Heat, leaving them available for other Alphas.

1

The sun hangs low in the sky, casting a warm, rosy glow over the sprawling garden at the swankiest hotel I've ever seen.

Chairs form two rows on either side of a stone walkway, leading up to a grotto where the wedding ceremony will take place, while paper lanterns hang like puffy clouds around the large space. The larger reception area off to the left holds a small stage where a live orchestra plays and an hors d'oeuvre table for the pre-wedding celebration.

Servers thread through the guests who have already arrived, passing out beverages and appetizers while an open bar offers the heavier stuff.

I pause at the top of the stairs, taking it all in.

Zac, the wedding organizer and my former foster

brother, had really flexed his billionaire status in renting out this place for our foster mother, Carrie, and her soon-to-be husband, Sean.

Nervous sweat coats my palms, and my pulse races with a mixture of excitement and anxiety. It's been eight years since I've been back to my hometown.

Now, surrounded by all these familiar faces from my foster home, it dredges up all the painful memories of what happened my senior year of high school. Even driving past the old football fields had brought on flashbacks of broken promises and unfulfilled dreams.

"Hey, Brad," a voice calls out, jarring me out of the messiness of being eighteen and out of control. "What are you doing hovering at the entrance, stranger?"

I turn to see Ben approaching with a grin that hasn't changed one bit. Beside him, Flinn beams at me, his freckle-covered cheeks bunching and his arm wrapped around Ben's waist.

"Hey, yourself!" I hurry down the stairs to pull the small man into a bear hug, then shake Flinn's hand. "You both look amazing."

Ben reaches out to squeeze my bicep. "You're not looking too shabby yourself."

"Thanks." I give a self-conscious laugh.

While I played football in high school, I quit when I went on to university. I'm still in pretty good shape, especially for an Omega, but nowhere near as bulky as I was the last time I saw my foster siblings.

"Did you check into your room yet?" Flinn asks. "We're on the third floor."

I pull the key card from my pocket to double check. "I'm on the first floor."

Yet another thing Zac went all out on. He booked rooms for all the guests, making it easy to arrive early enough to check in and change into my suit, so I didn't have to drive over while wearing it. It also removes the worry of staying too late, or having to remain sober or figure out a way home.

Not that my apartment is anywhere near here. I moved out of this town as soon as I graduated from high school. While I regretted leaving my foster family behind, I needed to put distance between me and my father, or I never would have been able to let go of all the negativity that surrounded him and found a semblance of peace.

"What time do you need to leave tomorrow?" Ben leans against Flinn's side. "Can you stay for brunch?"

I nod. "I have the whole weekend off."

After eight years of absence, part of me thinks I

should swing by my old house to see my dad while I'm here, too, but the thought tightens my stomach with anxiety. Our relationship, always rocky, had never recovered from the night he caught me with my first boyfriend.

The flood of my overhead light turning on makes me flinch, followed by the bang of my door crashing against the wall.

Rian jerks upright, squinting at my father, who stands in the door, his face turning purple as he takes in the situation.

I yank the blanket up to cover us. "Dad, I—"

He swipes a hand through the air to cut me off, and his angry gaze fixes on Rian. "That your car taking up my driveway?"

Rian swallows hard. "Yes, sir."

He steps into my room and points toward the door. "You best move it before the tow truck arrives to haul it off my property."

"Yes, sir." Rian's gaze jumps to me, his panic clear.

My hand shakes as I pull the blanket higher. "Just go."

Nodding, he scrambles from the bed and yanks on

his pants before grabbing the rest of his clothes and fleeing past my infuriated father.

I meet his angry gaze. "I thought you were working the night shift tonight."

"Clearly." He grabs my pants, throwing them at me. "Get dressed and pack a bag."

My stomach sinks. "Why?"

His face turns purple with rage. "You think you can bring guys home when I'm not around? Are you trying to get knocked up? Or do you just have no sense in that Omega brain of yours when it comes to Alphas?"

"It's not like that," I protest, Rian's feeling footsteps still echoing in the house. "We're in love."

My father barks out an ugly laugh. "Sure you are, up until he gets you pregnant and ditches your stupid ass. Well, I'm not raising another kid. So, get the hell out of my house."

"Dad." I shake my head. "You don't mean tha—"

"Get out!" he roars.

Tears sting my eyes. "But where will I go?"

"That's your problem, not mine." He stabs a finger toward the door. "You have five minutes to pack a bag, and then I want you out of my house!"

With that, he stomps from the room, slamming the door behind him.

2

My father's rage filled voice in my memory threatens to undo all the careful progress I've made over the years to make peace with being an Omega.

Is it worth risking a setback just to see if his views on Omegas have changed over time? I hadn't told him I would be in town, and I'm not sure I can force myself through a strained visit.

I shake my head, trying to dispel the memory. Today is about happiness and celebration, not the fucked-up things I went through in high school.

Sean and Carrie have touched so many lives with their kindness and acceptance. If not for Carrie, I would have never learned to stop seeing my Omega status as something to be ashamed of. I never would have gone to therapy or made peace with the fact that my father's views didn't define me as a person.

Ben touches my arm. "You okay, man?"

"Yeah, it's just been a long time since I've been home." I rub the sweat from the back of my neck. "What have you all been up to?"

As Ben lights up with excitement about a new comic collaboration he's doing with another artist named Basil Bark, the tension in my body melts away. He points out a guy with brown hair lingering near the stage, where his bond mate, Aster Woods, plays the violin.

As we chat more, Joshua appears, hand in hand with an older man, and I do a double take. "Is Joshua wearing a *suit*?"

I've never seen Joshua in anything but pajama bottoms. Of course, he was fifteen when we lived in the home together, but all of his social posts support that his habit hasn't changed in the near decade since then.

Ben's laughter jars me back to the present as he whips around and elbows his fiancé. "You owe me twenty dollars."

Flinn sighs and reaches into his pocket to pull out

his wallet and pass over the money. "Fine, but you're paying for the cab home."

Joshua spots us and ditches his date to race over and thrust his hand out toward Ben. "Give me my money."

Ben dutifully passes over the twenty.

Flinn gapes at his fiancé. "Seriously? That's cheating."

The older man joins our group, nods at us, and curls a hand around Joshua's shoulder. "Do you want anything to drink?"

Joshua holds out the twenty. "Get us some wine. My treat."

He tucks the money into Joshua's pocket and kisses his cheek. "It's an open bar, brat."

With another nod at us, the man strides toward the bar.

Joshua watches him go before turning to smirk at Ben. "Guess why we're late."

"No." Ben points a finger at him. "Stop right now."

My brows pinch together. "Did you guys have car problems?"

Flinn frantically shakes his head, his face blushing as red as his hair. "Don't encourage him. It's always dick related."

"No!" Ben wails and throws his arms around Joshua. "Not my innocent baby!"

"Get off!" Joshua protests, wiggling while not really attempting to escape. "It's your fault for convincing me to wear a suit. I look so hot that my *fiancé* couldn't keep his hands off me."

"Look at him bragging about being engaged after giving us shit for so long," Flinn grumbles.

Ben covers Joshua's ears. "Hush, or he'll try to move in with us again."

As I laugh at their antics, my anxiety over being here slips away. Despite the years, it feels like coming home, something that I've been missing for a long time.

A leggy, dark-haired woman joins us in a killer green dress. Samantha doesn't look all that different from the sleek, put-together girl I'd met back in high school. Then and now, people never would have thought she had anything except the perfect life.

Joshua and Samantha were the first people outside of Carrie and Sean to welcome me to the foster home. The first people my age who made me realize I wasn't completely alone.

. . .

A knock jolts me out of sleep, and I stare around at an unfamiliar bedroom in confusion.

Where am I? Did Rian and I go to an afterparty?

The knock comes again, followed by the sound of a door opening. "Hey, you better get in the shower now if you want a chance at it before you leave for school."

With a groan, I prop myself up on my elbow to see a young guy peeking into my room. The sight of his tousled black hair brings back the memories from last night.

Of me frantically packing my bag with tears streaming down my face.

Of my father's refusal to even look at me as I shuffled past him and out the front door.

The door opens wider, and the black-haired kid—Joshua, I remember—shuffles inside. He had been awake, hanging out in the kitchen, when I arrived at the foster home last night.

He still wears the pair of red-checkered fleece pajamas and an oversized blue hoodie from the night before as he stops near the closet. "Do you remember where you are?"

"Yeah." My voice comes out gruff from crying, and my swollen face hurts. "What about the shower? Sorry, I'm still waking up."

"Zac just got out, and Samantha has the time slot right before breakfast, so if you want to shower before

school, now's your chance." Curiosity lights his eyes as he stares at me. *"You can use any of the products in the shower. If you want to buy different ones, get a shower caddy, too, so you can take it in and out of the bathroom with you. If it's in the shower, it's free game."*

"Got it." I look around for my bag and spot it on the floor near an empty desk. "Thank you."

"Bathroom's the door near the stairs on the left." He backs out of my room. "I'm going to go sleep for a couple of hours."

I follow him out of the bedroom. "Don't you need to get ready, too?"

"I'm homeschooled, so while Carrie gets you all fed and shipped off, I get to sleep." He stifles a yawn. "Enjoy breakfast. Carrie's making French toast and bacon today."

At the words, the scent of cinnamon and sugar drifts to me from downstairs, and my stomach clenches with nausea. I love French toast, but I don't think I'll be able to keep anything down right now.

With a nod of thanks, I head into the bathroom, where steam still clings to the mirror.

Unsure how long I have before this Samantha person will be pounding on the door, I speed through my shower.

Only drying off enough to not be dripping wet, I

wrap a towel around my waist and hurry back out into the hall, where I crash into a tall, slender, dark-haired girl.

She drops the shower caddy she carries, and it crashes to the floor, spilling products everywhere.

"Sorry." I hold my towel in place as I crouch to help gather them back up.

"New arrival?" she asks as she grabs the conditioner that rolls toward the stairs.

"Yeah, I guess so." I drop a bottle of body spray into the caddy.

"That sucks." She grabs the caddy's handle and stands. "I'm sorry to see you here."

Startled, I straighten to stare at her. "What?"

"You're Brad Larson, from the football team." She thrusts out her hand. "Samantha Hamilton. Flintwood's senior class rep."

Recognition hits, and I shake her hand. "Damn. Sorry I didn't recognize you."

At school, her hair is always sleeked back, and she wears expensive clothes and makeup.

She releases my grip. "This isn't exactly the place you want to see a familiar face."

"Right."

I've gone to school with Samantha for nearly four years now, and it sucks to find out that someone I've admired has a shitty enough home life to end up here like me.

She offers me a smile. "Whatever got you sent here, I'm sorry. The world is a crappy place, but Carrie's good people. She'll make you feel at home."

Home? I'm not sure I know what that word means anymore.

3

"Brad, it's been way too long!" Samantha hurries over, her high heels making her almost as tall as me.

"Samantha." I hug her. "It's good to see you."

She steps back and lifts my hands, inspecting my ring finger before her eyes spot the nape guard peeking out of my collar. "Thank goodness you're still single. All these happy couples are giving me the hives."

"Don't be jealous." Joshua buffs his platinum band against his suit jacket. "You're at a wedding. Love is in the air, and your special someone could be here today."

"If anyone comes near me with hearts in their eyes, I'll stab them with an appetizer fork." Samantha links her arm through mine. "Come on, big and buff. Guard me from any love hounds while I hunt down that platter of stuffed mushrooms I saw earlier."

Laughing, I wave at the others as Samantha drags me through the crowd.

We find the server with the right platter, and Samantha hands me two, then takes two for herself, and we find an empty standing table near the edge of the patio.

I set the two small plates in front of her and lean against the table.

She glances around the garden. "Zac really pulled out all the stops for this wedding."

"He and Grant have enough experience at arranging them." Zac and his husband, Grant, have been married at least six times in the last few years, though I hadn't attended.

I'd been in university for the first two, and then couldn't get time off from work. But my newest promotion came with double the vacation days, so I can finally start socializing again.

"So, spill the tea." Samantha stuffs a mushroom into her mouth. "What's up with Brad?"

I laugh at her bluntness. "Nothing, really. Just working and paying bills. You?"

"I'm aiming for partner at my law firm." She

stuffs another mushroom into her mouth. "God, these are good. Think anyone will notice if I put some in my purse?"

I frown. "Didn't you get a full ride through law school? Why are you stealing food?"

Her green eyes narrow on me. "This dress cost me a fortune. All my clothes cost a fortune. I have to look like I belong next to all those high-profile clients, so I skimp where I can."

Wordlessly, I flag down another server passing by and take the entire tray of mushrooms from the man.

Grinning, Samantha pulls a tupperware container from her large purse. "Guard me."

I dutifully step in front of her, my back to the table to face the crowd as she uses my broad shoulders to hide her theft.

As I look around at all the loving couples, a pang of loneliness tugs at my heart. I try to push it aside, focusing on the cheerful atmosphere around me. Carrie has touched so many lives through her work with the Omega Outreach Program. The garden is packed with Omega kids from broken homes who she taught to trust again.

It's a testament to Carrie's efforts that there are so many couples at her wedding, when most Omegas who end up in the program have reason to fear relationships.

"Why are you single?" Samantha asks suddenly.

Surprised, I peer over my shoulder to see her stuffing her tupperware back into her purse. "What?"

She shrugs. "You're hot and doing good for yourself. Congratulations on your promotion, by the way. I got the email alert."

"Thanks." My stomach tightens.

She lifts her eyebrows. "So?"

I tug uncomfortably at my suit. "I'm not exactly the ideal Omega. A lot of Alphas are intimidated by me."

Not that I've tried hard to meet anyone. No one lives up to my first love, Rian, fellow footballer and the Alpha whose heart I broke. He's my biggest regret in life, and the one man I compare all others to.

Samantha's lips tighten, and she gives her head an angry shake. "Then they're stupid. You're a total catch."

I force a smile. "Right back at you. Aside from the whole threat of stabbing thing."

She throws back her head and laughs, drawing more than a few admiring gazes.

The signal for the wedding to begin cuts through the crowd, and Samantha grabs my arm, shoving me ahead of her toward the chairs. I put my big body to good use and break a path through the crowd to nab us chairs in the third row from the front.

The surrounding seats fill quickly, and I spot Joshua's fiancé in the front row sitting beside Dr. Walton, head of the OOP, and his husband, Herald, along with their three kids.

The music changes once more, and everyone stands, turning toward the back as the wedding party lines up.

The officiant walks down first, followed by Sean, who can't stop smiling, and no one here can blame him.

He courted Carrie for over a decade before she finally gave in and agreed to marry him. She had been hung up on their age difference, but anyone who saw them together knew they were in love.

Older couples follow behind him and split at the end, one sitting on either side of the aisle.

The bridesmaids and groomsmen file down next. Joshua comes in third, smirking at the crowd and waving like a little diva. The people closest to the aisle pelt him with rice-paper rose petals amid laughter from the crowd.

He takes his place next to Sean with an arm's length between them.

Then the best man and maid of honor step into the aisle, and my breath catches, my pulse racing.

Even after eight years, there's no mistaking Rian. My first love. He had filled out more after high school, and he wears his blond hair longer, but the dimples are still the same, as is the easy confidence with which he carries himself.

Time slows, and memories of our time together flood my mind. Our stolen moments, whispered promises, and the painful words I spoke that ended us.

Blood rushes in my ears, and my vision narrows until all I see is him.

As Rian draws nearer, his blue eyes meet mine. Our gazes lock, a storm of emotions swirling between us. My heart pounds, the years of separation tearing open an old wound and leaving me bleeding afresh.

Suddenly, I'm eighteen again, the crappy music from our senior-year Homecoming dance blaring in my ears with Rian's arms around me, desperately in love.

Music pounds through the gym, and students dance around us, bodies moving in jerky motions that attempt to match the beat. Laughter and chatter from the sidelines blend with the music, and the occasional cheers and whoops erupt, encouraging the more flamboyant dancers.

The school dance committee had done their best to transform the gym into a magical wonderland. The bleachers have been retracted to make room for the dance floor, and soft fairy lights strung across the ceiling twinkle down on us.

Large banners featuring the school's colors and the Homecoming theme hang on the walls, and tables draped in white paper tablecloths line the walls on both sides, adorned with fake, flickering candles.

The DJ's booth, placed at the far end, pulses with colorful lights.

Rian and I laugh as we knock against each other, arms in the air and bouncing to the beat of the base. Around us, members of the football team crowd together, their dates flushed and happy. Most had brought cheerleaders to the Homecoming dance, but a few had gone outside of the team, and those dates look stiffer than the rest, excited to be included but unsure if they belong in the group.

More cheers erupt as white smoke creeps along the floor, rising to surround us, and the DJ's voice blasts over the speakers. "Slow dance coming up next, so grab your dates and keep that arm's length between you guys! No grinding on the dance floor!"

Laughter rises, and our teammates grab their dates, yanking them close.

The lights dim, and the music slows to a romantic song about love.

Rian turns to me and tugs me against his big body.

Flushing, I glance at our teammates, but no one is paying any attention to us.

Rian's head dips toward mine, and his low rumble fills my ear. "Relax, Brad, you're here with me tonight, and no one is going to tell your dad."

I swallow hard and relax against him. We started dating two months ago, and our team knows, but I haven't been brave enough to tell my dad yet. My mom left before I was old enough to remember her, and he raised me by himself. When I was old enough, he pushed me to join all the team sports at school, wanting an athlete for a son.

He hadn't taken my status as an Omega well.

Over the years, he calmed down about it, but I still catch him making remarks about the trouble with Omegas. Like he just blocks that his own son is an Omega from his mind.

Bringing home an Alpha boyfriend just wouldn't go over well in our house, so I asked Rian to keep it a secret, at least until I can get a scholarship for football to the local university.

Once I'm out of my dad's house, we can be as open about our relationship as Rian wants.

Soft lips brush my neck, and I shiver in response. We haven't done more than sneak quick make-out sessions behind the gym and a couple of hand jobs, and we're both growing impatient with the self-restraint.

Heart pounding, I turn my head at the same time that Rian lifts his, and our mouths meet. At the feel of his chapped lips and the wet warmth of his tongue as it gently sweeps into my mouth, my eyes flutter closed. He tastes like fruit punch and breath mints, which is my new favorite combination.

His hand slips under my suit jacket to cup my waist, and a whimper escapes at the heat of his hand against me, with only the thin barrier of my dress shirt separating us.

A throat clears loudly from next to us, followed by the hard prod of a ruler. "Three foot rule, boys."

We hastily step back, straightening our arms, and the chaperone nods before she moves on to prod at another couple who are doing far more than kissing.

Rian's lips twitch, and a giggle escapes me.

As soon as the teacher vanishes from view, he pulls me back in. "Hey, want to get out of here?"

I nod quickly, and he catches my hand, dragging me off the dance floor, then out of the gym.

The bright lights of the hall blind me, and I don't resist when he presses me up against a set of lockers, his mouth sliding over mine once more. His hands drop to my ass, tugging our hips flush, and another shiver goes through me when at the press of his hard length against mine.

My ass clenches as I imagine him sliding inside me, of finally being with him.

"I love you, Brad," he whispers against my ear. "I want to be with you so bad right now."

With a groan, I rock my hips against his. "Me, too."

His mouth moves to my neck, sucking my racing pulse and sending shivers of pleasure through me. "Your dad's working the night shift tonight, right?"

Lust clouds my thoughts. "Yeah."

He catches my earlobe and bites gently. "Which means your house is empty, right?"

With a moan, my eyes close. "Yeah."

His hands move on my ass, his fingers digging in my crease. "That means we won't get caught if we go there, right?"

"Yeah," I moan, nearly coming in my pants.

His head lifts, and his green eyes search mine. "Yeah?"

Nervousness hits me when I realize what I agreed to. But he's right. My dad won't be home until morning, and I'm desperate to be with Rain.

I hook my fingers into his belt. "You have to leave before he gets home at four in the morning."

4

An elbow in my ribs jars me from the memory just in time to hear the words, "You may now kiss the bride."

I stand and clap with everyone else, tears stinging my eyes, both from the memory of what could have been and the joy of seeing two of my favorite people happy together.

Carrie blushes as Sean sweeps her into his arms and kisses her with a passion that can't be denied.

"Whoo!" Samantha puts her fingers to her lips and lets out a loud whistle. "About damn time!"

Similar cheers rise from those around me, and good-natured laughs fill the air.

Samantha hugs me, her shrieks of happiness

splitting my eardrums, and I cup my hands around my mouth to wolf howl.

The couple separates, Sean beaming proudly and Carrie flustered but happy.

The wedding officiant clasps their hands and raises them into the air. "I present to you, Mr. And Mrs. Buckley."

More cheers follow, and as the happy couple walks back down the aisle, we throw rice paper flower petals into the air.

Then the wedding party passes, too, and my eyes meet Rian's once more. My heart thuds painfully, my breath catching in my throat. After several heartbeats, he looks away and passes our seats, continuing down the aisle.

Samantha squeezes my arm, her voice pitched to reach my ear through the cheering crowd. "Did you know he'd be here?"

I shake my head. "I didn't even know Sean knew him."

"He must be related to be part of the wedding party." She shakes her head. "Talk about a small world."

Yeah, small world.

. . .

There was nothing good about being an Omega, and being kicked out of my home just solidified that fact in my mind.

I was lucky to find a twenty-four-hour diner to hang out in the first night, sipping coffee until morning. For Saturday night, I used my meager savings to rent a room at a crappy motel.

In my mad scramble to get out of the house, I'd left behind my cell, so I used the phone at the motel to call my dad, but he hadn't answered.

Despair set in after that. I only had enough for one night, and I couldn't even call Rian, because I didn't have his number memorized,

But that was probably for the best.

What could I say? There was no way I could stay with him, and a part of me was angry that he had even suggested we go back to my house.

He knew *my dad didn't like that I was an Omega. If he hadn't suggested we sneak into my room, we never would have been caught, and I wouldn't be homeless now.*

On Sunday night, I was lucky that Sean found me and took me to Carrie's foster home.

In all the chaos, though, I miss morning practice on Monday.

When I arrive at the football field, it's deserted, but I find Coach in his office.

My knock on the door brings his head up, and he scowls. "Larson, you missed practice."

My shoulders hunch. "Yes, Coach."

His hard eyes narrow on me. "What's your excuse?"

He doesn't know about the OOP, and I'm too ashamed to tell him. "I overslept."

"Well, put on your gear and start running laps," he snaps.

I swallow the lump forming in my throat. "I don't have my gear, Coach."

Yet another thing I didn't think to grab while my life was falling apart.

He closes his laptop and stares at me. "What's going on, Larson? You never miss practice, and now you show up late with no gear?"

My eyes sting, and I blink quickly. "I lost my gear, Coach."

"Lost it?" At my nod, he sits back in his chair. "How soon can you replace it?"

I shrug. Everything I had I spent on that one night at the motel. Can the OOP help me buy replacement gear? I should have asked Carrie about that this morning, but there was so much already happening.

Coach folds his hands. "If you miss two more

practices without gear, I'll have to bench you for the next game, and you know what that means."

I nod. If my replacement, Hendricks, does well, Coach could decide to make him primary and keep me on the bench for the rest of the season. Hendricks has been gunning for my position, and if I'm benched, it will cost me any chance at getting a football scholarship to university.

"Well, get going then," Coach says gruffly. "Don't be late for your class."

Nodding again, I leave his office and stride down the hall.

As I pass the locker rooms, Rian steps out, his hair wet from his shower, and that queasy knot in my stomach tightens.

His eyes widen with surprise before he lurches forward to grab my shoulders. "Brad, where have you been? I tried calling all weekend. Why didn't you answer? What happened? Why weren't you at practice today?"

His Alpha pheromones curl around me, demanding that I lean into him, that I let him fix everything that's happened.

But that's what got me into this mess to begin with. I trusted Rian, and now my life is trashed.

The anger and resentment that had grown over the

weekend bubbles and festers. Part of me knows that we both agreed to go back to my house, that hormones had been driving our decisions, but I can't make the resentment go away.

If not for Rian, I never would have given in to temptation, and I wouldn't now be homeless, facing down the end of any dreams I had of playing university-level football.

I shake off his hands. "Don't touch me."

Shock crosses his face. "Brad?"

"Just stay away from me." I turn and storm down the hall.

He catches up, spinning me around. "What's going on, baby? What happened? You can tell me."

I try to shrug him off. "I can't be around you anymore. We're over."

"But…" His desperate eyes search my face. "Didn't Friday night mean anything to you? We were each other's firsts. My bite is still on your neck."

"I wasn't in Heat, so it will go away." I look away from him, my throat burning. "Everything needs to just go away."

"Baby, what happened?" He tries to pull me into his arms. "Did you dad—"

"I said, don't touch me!" I shove him backward, my chest heaving. "Don't ever touch me again. We're done!"

Tears fill his eyes. "But I love you."

"That's your problem, not mine!" Turning away from his stricken expression, I storm out onto the field.

5

After I broke up with Rian, we'd avoided each other at practice, which wasn't hard with me running laps or practicing with the backup players. My fear had proven real when Hendricks took my primary spot on the team, and I'd only played one more game my senior year.

It had turned out to be a blessing in disguise, making me realize I had only joined football because my father pressured me into proving I could still be manly, despite my Omega status. I had stuck with it through high school graduation but focused more on my classes, and the OOP helped me get a scholarship to an out-of-town university.

Away from my father, I discovered what I really wanted in life, and I graduated with a degree in journalism. I've worked with a news channel for a while, writing sports articles for their online subscription.

It's hard work, but I finally received a promotion that allows for more time off, and the blog I started as a side project has gotten enough traction that I could go independent soon.

My boss is aware of it and had pulled me into her office before I left for the wedding to discuss options for a more flexible work schedule that will allow me to work from home. As long as I turn in my articles on time, I won't have to work the standard nine to five, freeing up my options.

We're supposed to talk about it more when I return to work on Monday and do a trial run. It would be nice to keep my benefits and have my travel expenses covered while pursuing my other interests with my blog.

I finally feel like my life is in a good place. But seeing Rian again reminds me of one of my biggest regrets. I was hurting and lashed out at Rian, blaming him for something that wasn't his fault, and I need to apologize for that, if he'll let me.

I just never thought I'd be given the chance to make amends at my foster mom's wedding.

Once the wedding party leaves, the guests disperse

to the reception area, making room for the staff to clear the seats and set up the dance floor.

Samantha and I rejoin Ben, Flinn, and the older gentleman who came with Joshua, who introduces himself as Austen. I spot Elijah, Flinn's best friend, weaving through the guests with his camera, snapping pictures.

More hors d'oeuvres come out, and I grab extra plates for Samantha without being asked.

"These are so good." She stuffs a cracker into her mouth. "Who's catering this shindig?"

"A local cafe owned by Warren Markham." Flinn tips his head toward a man near the cake table who's so pregnant he looks ready to pop. "He's family friends with Zac and Dr. Walton."

Past the cake table, I spot the wedding party gathering on the well-manicured lawn for pictures, and Rian draws my gaze once more.

He looks good, even after all the years that have passed. Like me, he's lost some of the football bulk, but his body still fills out his suit in all the right places. His hair, longer than it was in high school, curls around his ears, and a light beard defines his square jaw.

I'd be a liar if I said he didn't make my pulse

quicken, both with nerves and that small part of me that never stopped loving him.

The memory of our last time together crashes over me.

Rian breaks every speed limit as he drives us from the Homecoming dance to my house.

At the front door, I fumble with my keys to open the door, then lead him through the dark house to my bedroom.

Since I hadn't planned to bring anyone here tonight, I didn't pick up before I left earlier, so I leave off the lights and draw him toward my small twin bed.

His hands shake as he pushes off my jacket, then unbuttons my shirt, peppering kisses over my face and down my throat to my shoulders as he bares them.

My pulse races like crazy as I do the same for him, sweeping my hands over his muscular pecs and abs. When I reach for his belt, his stomach contracts on a sharp intake of breath. I open his buckle and zipper, then push his slacks down to leave him standing in only his boxers.

Light from the window illuminates his fit form, and my eyes greedily drink him in. It's not the first time I've seen him in his boxers—hell, I've seen him naked in the locker room—but now I get to touch and taste, to feel that hard body on top of mine, and it nearly makes me come on the spot.

Rian pushes me back onto the bed, and I land on my elbows, watching as he kneels in front of me to take care of my pants. Despite how big he is, his fingers tremble when they undo my fly, and I lift my hips to make it easier to take off my pants.

He tosses them aside and leans over me to press his lips against my stomach. "I love you so much, Brad."

My fingers in his short, blond hair. "I love you, too, Rian."

He crawls onto the bed over me, and I fall back, my head on my pillow and legs spread wide. Every instinct in my body tells me this is my Alpha, the only one meant for me.

His lips find mine once more, and he grinds our hips together, our hard lengths rubbing together through the fabric of our boxers. It's a good thing we have all night to get this right, because I won't last long the first time. Not at the rate we're going.

I wrap my legs around Rian's hips and grip his ass, encouraging him to keep going as pleasure curls up my spine and my balls tighten.

He groans against me. "I want to Mark you so bad. Want to make it so all the world knows you're mine."

I draw his mouth to my throat. "Make me yours."

6

"If you keep staring like that, people are going to notice," Samantha whispers.

Cheeks warming, I jerk my eyes away from Rian.

After so many years, we're not the same men who fumbled around in dark corners, stealing moments between classes and practice. I don't know what he's been up to in the last eight years, what kind of person he's become, and I don't have the right to want to know.

Maybe trying to talk to him here is a bad idea. If he's still angry about how things ended between us, it could cause a scene, and I don't want to disrupt Carrie's wedding.

I turn to Samantha. "I should stay away from

him."

Her eyebrows arch. "Why?"

"What if he hates me?" My hands tremble with anxiety, and I shove them into my pockets. "I don't want to risk causing a scene at Carrie's wedding."

"I can respect that." She snatches a cracker with some kind of stinky cheese off my plate and stuffs it into her mouth. "Closure is overrated, anyway."

Wow, way to make me feel like a coward while validating my decision. "Are you trying to use reverse psychology on me?"

"Nope." She takes my plate from me. "Not every pain needs to be dug up and poked at. If you're okay with how things ended, then leave it buried."

"What's this about burying?" Joshua slips past me to smash his small body against Austen's side. "Are we planning a murder?"

"No murder," I rush to tell him, because Joshua is definitely the type of friend who would grab a shovel to make a body disappear.

"Hey, Joshua." Samantha fixes her eyes on him. "Who's the best man?"

"Rian?" Joshua glances toward the dance floor. "He's Sean's nephew." His gaze returns to us, and he frowns. "Didn't you all go to Flintwood together?"

"Oh, right, he was on the football team."

Samantha gives me wide eyes. "Weren't you on the football team, too?"

"Shut up," I hiss at her.

"You guys are being weird." Joshua tugs on Austen's tie. "Go fetch me more booze. Standing in front of all those people was horrible."

"Don't get too drunk tonight." Austen's hand curls around the back of Joshua's neck. "I have plans for you and this suit later."

Joshua licks his lips as he stares up at the man. "I give you permission to take advantage of me while I'm intoxicated."

Ben whimpers. "That's my child saying those nasty things."

Flinn pats his head. "There, there."

As soon as Austen heads toward the bar, Joshua turns to us. "Guess what I got in the mail yesterday?"

"What?" Samantha asks, her eyes gleaming with interest.

"No." Ben covers his eyes. "I don't want to know."

Joshua peers over his shoulder to check Austen's location before pulling his shirt from his pants to reveal a black and gold silk corset cinching in his already trim waist. "Lady B sent it to me. It's going to lock in the deal for Austen to finally launch the Men at Night line. I put it on after Austen ravished me earlier."

Ben whimpers and pretends to faint against his fiancé's side.

"Hey, is that from Lady B?" Elijah asks, coming in at the end of the conversation. "That matches the one you gave us for Dominick."

I vaguely remember that Dominick Steel is a male lingerie model and Elijah's boyfriend. Austen must be in the same field.

"Hey, can we get one, too?" Flinn flinches when Ben rises from his faint and hits him. "What? You wore the lace—"

He cuts off when Ben hits him again before stepping across the circle to join Samantha and me, and the lingerie fanatics huddle up together.

I turn toward Samantha just in time for her to abandon for the other group, leaving me and Ben alone.

I glance at him. "So…"

Ben glares at the newly formed clique. "Never try on a pair of lace underwear around your partner unless you want to wear it for the rest of your life, man. Flinn never had an interest in this stuff until I let Joshua talk me into trying on a pair of sexy briefs."

I chuckle awkwardly. "I don't think that will be a problem. Lingerie isn't built for my body type."

"You've obviously never seen Dominick Steel's social page." Ben pulls out his phone and opens an app.

He turns the screen toward me, displaying a strong-figured man in lingerie. The lace teddy he wears serves to highlight his muscular frame, while his long, blond hair drapes artfully over his broad shoulders.

This is Elijah's boyfriend? No wonder he didn't even blink at Joshua displaying a modest corset.

Blood rushes to my cheeks, and I look away. "I don't think I'd have the confidence for something like that, but good for him."

Ben tucks his phone away. "What was Samantha playing at with the whole Rian thing? Didn't you guys date briefly in high school? Is she just poking fun at you?"

"We were trying to figure out how he was related to Sean." My eyes drift back to the dance floor. "It was a bit of a shock seeing him here."

"Yeah, I was surprised when I found out they were related, too." Ben glances over at Rian. "He's been helping at the foster home recently. He's considering signing up to work as personal security,

Love at Last

so he's been shadowing Sean and Flinn to see what the job entails."

It surprises me to hear Rian would be interested in that kind of job. What happened to his dream of going pro?

"You should go talk to him," Ben says.

Startled, I tear my eyes away from Rian. "What?"

"It's obviously going to bother you until you do." Ben nudges me. "Now's the time, before they get into the cake cutting and first dance. He'll be busy then."

I swallow hard. Is now really a good time? Do I really want to rip open this old wound? Rian is alone right now, so this may be my only chance.

With a deep breath, I straighten my shoulders and stride toward the dance floor.

Rian spots me coming right away and stiffens. His eyes dart to the side, but he doesn't turn and leave, which I take as a good sign.

My heart pounds as I stop in front of him. "Hey."

"Hey," he says, his hand tightening on the wine glass he holds.

Silence fills the space between us as we stare at each other.

"Well, this is awkward." I chuckle and rub the back of my neck. "Do you have a second to go somewhere and talk?"

His eyes dart to the side again. "Why? I didn't think you wanted anything to do with me."

My gut clenches at hearing my words from all those years ago thrown back at me, but I deserve it. I hurt Rian, and I have no right to ask for his time now.

I drop my hand back to my side. "Look, I just wanted to say that I'm sorry for what happened in high school. I was in a bad place, and—"

"There you are!" a slender man slips between us, taking the glass of wine from Rian and linking their arms together with a familiarity that makes my gut twist. "Sorry I kept you waiting. There was a line for the restroom."

Blood rushes through my ears as my gaze fixes on their linked arms. Of course, Rian would be here with someone. Or worse, is this his *partner*? Are they bonded?

My eyes rise to the man's collar, but I can't see a nape guard past the elaborate scarf tied around his neck.

The other man's gaze shifts to me. "Who's this?"

Rian's eyes bounce between the slender man to me. "Brad, this is my—"

"Sorry to bother you," I croak out, not wanting to hear the confirmation that they're an item. "I just wanted to…" I flounder for words. "Enjoy the wedding."

Rian calls after me, but I stumble away, unable to hear his words past the crush of disappointment that floods through me.

Samantha was right. I should have left this buried.

Whoever said time heals all wounds was full of shit. This hurts just as much as it did eight years ago.

7

Samantha intercepts me as I blindly walk away from the dance floor. "Hey, what happened?"

I swallow the lump in my throat. "I need to go to my room. Staying here... I can't do this right now."

"Keep it together for just a little longer." Gripping my arm, she pulls me over to one of the standing tables beside the champaign tower. She thrusts a flute into my numb fingers before grabbing the other one on the table. "The bride and groom are about to enter."

Guilt fills me, and I take a healthy gulp of bubblies to fortify myself. Today isn't about me and my regrets. It's about people who are far better than I am.

Zac, who stands next to the champaign tower, gently taps a fork against the flute he holds. Silence falls over the room, then a processional song fills the air, and Carrie and Sean appear at the top of the stairs.

Carrie had changed out of her full-skirted wedding dress into a sleeker version to make dancing easier, while Sean had taken off his jacket and tie. The couple steals loving glances at each other as they walk down the stairs, and we all raise our champagne glasses as cheers fill the air.

As soon as they pass, I drain the rest of my glass before stealing Samantha's and drinking it, too.

Without comment, she grabs two fresh flutes from the table beside us.

Carrie and Sean make their way to the long table on the other side of the champagne tower and take their seats. Joshua abandons Austen to join them, and my stomach clenches when I spot Rian leaving his date to sit in the chair beside Sean.

Sean takes the mic Zac passes him and stands with Carrie, the two holding hands.

He clears his throat, the sound crackling through the speakers set up around the reception area. "Thank you, everyone, for being here with us today, to celebrate this important milestone in our lives. Each of you has touched a place in our hearts, and today wouldn't have been the same without our loved ones surrounding us."

Tears flow down Carrie's cheeks, and she dabs at them with a napkin as she nods.

My own eyes sting, and I catch Samantha blinking quickly. I dare say they've both impacted our lives far more than we've touched theirs.

Joshua takes the microphone from Sean and waits for him and Carrie to sit. "Sean was the first face I remember after I lost my family, and Carrie's was the first hug that felt like home. I stayed the longest at our foster home, so I witnessed all of Sean's bumbling attempts at courtship and got to watch Carrie fall head over heels for him. It was awkward and took forever, but they finally admitted their feelings for each other, and I just have one thing to say."

He turns to look down at the laughing couple. "About damn time."

Hoots and whistles fill the air, and Carrie throws her napkin at him.

As Joshua passes the mic to Zac, the laughter quiets.

Zac raises the mic to his lips. "The home Carrie provided gave me a port in the storm after losing my parents. I can honestly say that, without the OOP, I would not be here today, standing next to my husband."

He touches the slight swell of his pregnant belly before reaching out to take the hand of the man who stands beside him. "Carrie didn't know my background or how important it was for me to hide from my aunts and uncles. All she knew was that I was in need, and that was enough for her to open her heart and her home to me. Thank you, both, for being there for me. With each other, you have found the harbor where you belong, filled with love for many years to come. Congratulations."

More tears stream down Carrie's cheeks, and she presses her hand over her heart.

Ben steps forward to take the mic. "Sean was my ride to Carrie's home, and I will never forget the fear and anxiety that filled me that night. But he and Carrie made sure I felt safe, something I no longer had with my family. The OOP protected me, but it was Carrie who gave me a new home when mine failed me, and I will forever be grateful for all the love and support I had there. The two of you built all of us a foundation with love, but now it's you who get to live in that home."

He wipes his eyes and holds the microphone out to Samantha, who fumbles to take it.

Her hand shakes slightly as she raises it to her lips. "Family didn't have meaning for me until I met Carrie. She taught me what real love was and that I held worth beyond my second gender. I love you. Keep making her happy for all of us, Sean."

She thrusts the microphone into my hands and chugs her champagne.

Unprepared, I lift the mic, my heart pounding and my thoughts slightly fizzy with champagne. "Sean found me walking the streets in the middle of the night after my dad kicked me out for being an Omega."

Beside Sean, Rian's eyes widen, but I force my focus to stay on the happy couple, afraid I'll lose it otherwise. "I could have died that night, because I didn't know who Sean was or even ask why he wanted me to get into his car. I was scared and took the first kind offer that came my way. Luckily, he didn't turn out to be a serial killer."

I pause while people laugh. "Sean drove me to Carrie's house, and through them, I learned that being an Omega wasn't something to be ashamed of. That there could be power in embracing who I am. But it took time for that lesson to sink in, and I burned my life down before I figured it out. I hurt people, my friends…my boyfriend."

I swallow the lump threatening to cut off my words. "The OOP is about more than shelter against the world. It's a place to find acceptance, and to find a family. When I returned to my father's house, things didn't automatically get better. But when shit inevitably hit the fan, I always knew that Sean was a phone call away, and that Carrie's door would always be open. Thank you, both, for your patience and love. I'm so happy that you found love together. A better couple doesn't exist."

I scrub my eyes with a napkin as I pass the microphone to the person beside me. They tell their story, but I can't hear it through the rush of blood in my ears.

As soon as everyone's focus is far enough from me to make it possible, I escape the reception, fleeing into the hotel for a few minutes alone to regain my composure.

As I near my door, I fumble the keycard from my pocket and slide it into the lock.

"Brad, wait!" Rian's voice cuts through the pounding of my heart, and I glance back to see him running down the hall toward me.

Pulse racing, I shake my head as I shove my door open. I can't do this right now. As much as I want to apologize, I can't stand in front of the man who stole my heart so many years ago and pretend he doesn't still own it.

I stumble into my room, but Rian catches the door before it closes, coming inside uninvited.

Rian's intense blue eyes lock on me as he stalks forward. "I need to hear what you wanted to say earlier."

My throat clicks as I swallow and look away. If he needs to hear my apology again, it's the least he deserves. "I'm sorry that I hurt you back in high school. I was in a bad place, but that doesn't make up for how I treated you. You didn't deserve my anger. I just wanted you to know it had nothing to do with you and everything to do with what was going on in my life."

The words fall from my tongue with a sense of relief. I've practiced so many times what I would say to Rian if I ever had the chance, and releasing them leaves me lightheaded. Whether Rian accepts my apology is up to him, but I at least tried.

Gentle fingers touch my chin, drawing my gaze to his. "Why didn't you just tell me? What you said back there… That was the night of the dance, wasn't it? Why didn't you come to me?"

The pain in his voice tugs at my heart. "Everything happened so fast, and I didn't grab my phone, so I had no way of calling. And I couldn't just show up at your house. Not with how much your family already struggled. By the time Monday rolled around, I was past shock and deep into anger, blaming everyone around me for what happened. I'm sorry, you didn't deserve that."

"And you didn't deserve to lose your home just because I was horny and not thinking straight." He pushes my hair behind my ears, his touch burning with the memory of all the touches that came before. "I knew how your father was. I should never have suggested we go back to your place."

A weak laugh escapes me. "You weren't the only one letting hormones make decisions that night. The thing with my dad was going to happen at some point, no matter what. He was always going to resent me for being a weak Omega."

"But you weren't weak." Rian steps closer, his eyes dropping to my mouth. "You were never weak. I'm sorry I didn't realize you were in pain. I should have been there for you. Should have pushed harder to figure out what was wrong."

"I wouldn't have let you back then." My breaths quicken at his nearness, and I lick my lips. "You have nothing to apologize for."

He reaches out to grip my waist, pulling me

forward until our bodies press together. "I've never stopped thinking about you, Brad."

I lift a hand to his chest, and his heart thunders beneath my palm. "Wait."

"Why?" His hand moves to the back of my head, tangling in my curls. "Your heart is racing just as fast as mine."

My pulse pounds faster, and my eyes drop to his mouth as the memory of how good it felt to kiss him floods through me.

A low rumble rises from his chest, melting away the last of my resistance, and he closes the distance between our lips. His kiss tastes bittersweet, of broken promises and shattered hearts. It burns with memories of our younger selves, of the recklessness that drove us together and ultimately broke us apart.

I melt against him, chasing the dreams shared and the paths not taken, our lips moving together in a dance half-forgotten but remembered by our bodies.

He steps forward, pressing me against the wall, his mouth slanting over mine to deepen the kiss. His hands drop to my ass, tugging our hips flush, and a shiver goes through me at the hard press of his cock against mine.

It's high school all over again, my body desperate

to become one with him, for this Alpha to claim me as his Omega.

But then my eyes open, and the harsh lights of my hotel room remind me that this Alpha already belongs to another, and the fire dies inside me.

With a hard shove, I push Rian away from me, my chest heaving. "Stop. Stop touching me."

"Why?" He lunges forward, ripping open the collar of my shirt, and a satisfied growl escapes him when he sees my nape guard. "You're not claimed. If there's someone already in your life, forget them. I'll overwrite any Mark you have. You're mine."

"No, I'm not. This is all getting confused." I push him back once more before his pheromones make me forget why I can't have him. "You need to leave. Archie will be looking for you."

The other man's name burns my lips, and every fiber of my being screams that Archie doesn't matter, that if Rian wants me, that means he's not bonded yet.

But I can't ruin Rian's life just because my body yearns to be joined with his.

Swallowing hard, I point toward the door. "I apologized. Now, please leave before something happens that you'll regret."

8

"Archie?" Rian shakes his head. "What does he have to do with us?"

"He's your *date*," I say, hating the word on my lips.

Rian barks out a laugh. "He's my *cousin*."

My arm drops back to my side. "What?"

"Didn't you hear me introduce you earlier?" Rian crowds back into my personal space and spins the small dials on my nape guard, unlocking it. He takes it off and tosses it toward the bathroom. "You really shouldn't use your birthday for something this important."

Cool air brushes against the bare skin around my neck, and I look up at him in confusion. "What are you—"

A gasp escapes me when he spins me around and tugs down the back of my shirt, exposing my nape.

"Good, no Mark." He leans in to press his lips against the sensitive place at the base of my neck, sending a shiver of awareness down my spine. "I'm glad I don't have to fight off another Alpha."

His weight leaves my back, and before I know what's happening, he spins me back around and pushes me onto the queen-sized bed.

I land with a bounce, the bright lights of the hotel room flooding down around us. This is the exact opposite of the nervous fumbling we did in high school, and it leaves my mind reeling.

"Not that I wouldn't fight to claim you." Rian tugs off his tie as he moves to stand between my spread legs. "But it makes it easier knowing there's no one meaningful standing in my way."

Heart racing, I push up onto my elbows and watch him strip out of his suit jacket, tossing it aside. "Don't you think you're moving a little fast?"

He bends to cup the front of my slacks, where my flagging erection presses against my zipper, and I harden instantly. "It doesn't feel like I'm moving fast enough. We have a lot of time to make up for. I still love you, Brad. No matter how hard I tried, those feelings never went away. You've always been the one for me."

The heat of his palm against me makes it hard to focus on his words. "We don't even know each other anymore."

"I just moved back to town and am floating between jobs while I decide what I want to do with my life." He pops the button open on my slacks and drags down the zipper, his fingers stroking my hard length along the way. "I'm leaning toward working with my uncle, Sean, in the security business. I'm single, have had no significant relationships since high school, and I plan to get married and breed a ton of babies soon. You?"

Desire slicks my entrance, and my ass clenches in response. "Soon? How soon?"

He kneels between my knees to tug off my shoes, then reaches up to grip my waistband. "When's your Heat?"

"Not for a few weeks." My ass bounces on the bed as he yanks my pants and underwear off, and my heavy dick slaps against my stomach, leaving a wet spot of pre-cum on my happy trail. "But I'm on suppressants."

He pushes my legs wider and cups my balls. "Relationships?"

"Just random hookups." My head falls back, and I moan as he massages my sensitive sack. "And I'm about to go remote with my job."

"So you're not tied down. That's good." He grips one knee and shoves it toward my chest, exposing my slick entrance. "I don't know if I can be gentle the first time. Not with how long I've been dreaming of this pretty little hole."

More slick flows out of my entrance in response. With my body type, no one has ever made me feel small, and even the random guys I hooked up with all expected me to dominate, despite my Omega status.

But the way Rian handles me leaves no question about who's in charge, and the knowledge he can easily manhandle me into whatever position he wants sends desire coursing through me.

"You don't have to be gentle," I gasp, my pulse pounding. "I can take it."

Rian groans as he reaches for his zipper, dragging it down. His boxes tent out of the front of his slacks, and he moves them aside to free his cock.

Fisting it, he rubs the plump head against my entrance, slicking himself in my desire before he thrusts in to the hilt. I groan at the burn of being stretched open so suddenly, my inner muscles spasming around his thick shaft.

Gripping my leg harder, he withdraws, then slams home again, our moans mingling with the wet slap of our flesh coming together with each quick, hard thrust.

Rian straddles my thigh, then lifts my other leg onto his shoulder, turning me onto my side and spreading me open. The change in angle brings him deeper on the next thrust, and I cry out as he hits that bundle of nerves deep inside me.

With a satisfied growl, he holds me in place as his cock pistons in and out of my body, nailing my sweet spot over and over again. My balls grow heavy, my legs trembling.

"That's right." Rian thrusts deep and rolls his hips. "Come for me."

My toes curl, my back arching, and my dick pulses cum onto the comforter.

Rian pulls out, then slams home a final time, rocking his hips as his cock twitches and jumps inside me, pumping hot cum into my channel.

Breathing heavily, he drops my leg off his shoulder, his fat cock dragging from my body, still semi-hard. Rolling me onto my back once more, and he finishes tugging me out of my clothes while I'm still catching my breath.

Then he strips out of his own clothes, revealing a

powerful body still heavy with muscle. With ease, he maneuvers us fully onto the bed, and his body covers mine.

"Say it again," I gasp. "What you said earlier."

"I said a lot of things earlier, baby," he rumbles, the vibrations easing through my body, melting me beneath him. "But if you mean the part about how I never stopped loving you, I'll say that as many times as you need to hear it. I'm not letting you go again. I love you."

His lips slide down to my racing pulse. "I love you."

His teeth scrape against my skin. "I love you."

He bites down hard without breaking the skin, then licks the sting. "I love you."

Pleasure shoots through me, and my knees lift to curl around his hips, my body angling to take him in again. "I love you, too, Rian. So much. You're the only Alpha I want to Mark me. The only one I want to pin me down."

"God, baby, you're killing me." He works his semi-hard cock into my body, his hips pressing flush to mine to stay inside without moving, wanting to be joined with me as much as I yearn to be one with him. "I want to stay like this forever."

"Me, too." I wrap my arms around his big body,

marveling at the way we still fit perfectly together. "Always."

He nuzzles the bruise he left on my throat before rising to claim my lips in a languid kiss.

Slowly, his cock hardens inside me, and he claims me gently, the franticness of our first joining giving way to a soft exploration of lips and hands as we learn the map of bodies both familiar but changed by the time we spent apart.

Later, we force ourselves out of bed and help each other dress before returning to the party.

We missed the cake-cutting and the first dance, but make it in time for the bouquet toss.

Joshua surprises no one when he shoves his way to the front and nabs the victory, then struts it over to his amused fiancé while Flinn protests that the flowers were heading right toward Ben.

Rian reintroduces me to his cousin, and then we congratulate Carrie and Sean on their wedding once more.

When I wave farewell to my friends, I make no promises to be awake in time for brunch in the morning. At the rate they're throwing back alcohol, I won't be the only one who sleeps through the get-together, and I make plans to meet up with them later in the day.

Then Rian and I sneak away from the dancing, just like we did in high school, but with no one to hold us back this time.

Since he's sharing a room with his cousin, he whisks me back to mine, where we hang the *Do Not Disturb* sign on the handle before locking ourselves inside.

We have a lot to catch up on from the eight years we spent apart, but tonight, it's all about our reunion.

EPILOGUE

I take the heavy box from Rian's arms. "Here, I can get that. You grab the bag with the pillows."

He scowls down at me. "I can carry heavy things. Or do you need me to throw you over my shoulder again?"

Warmth creeps up my cheeks at the reminder of what we did last weekend. "That's why I want you to save your strength. If you hurt your knee moving me into your apartment, then we can't have fun on our first night living together."

Over the last several months, Rian and I have spent a lot of time on the phone and visiting over the weekends, getting to know each other again. I had learned he blew out his knee the first year of university football, ruining his chances of going pro, and that it still bothers him years later.

While he doesn't have a limp, he ices it on bad days, and I don't want to risk hurting him when I have plenty of lighter things he can carry.

A wolfish smile spreads over Rian's lips, and he leans down to growl into my ear. "I like where your priorities lie."

Grabbing the bag of pillows, he strides for the open door to his ground-floor apartment.

It had taken longer than I wanted for my job to approve me going remote, but the second the paperwork went through, I started packing to move back to my hometown. Rian already rents a two-bedroom apartment, and he offered his second bedroom for my office space.

I follow Rian into the apartment, which has become like a second home to me during my frequent trips back here.

Rian stands next to the couch, the bag he brought in open. "Are you sure we need so many pillows? We only have one couch, and with the other pillows you bought, there's barely room for us to sit."

"Don't judge my love of pillows." I drop the box I carry in the spare bedroom, where my new desk already waits for my computer. "I need every single one of them."

"Fine, but if they get in the way of me snuggling you, they're going in the dumpster." He upends the bag, and pillows tumble out onto the couch.

While he struggles to make them all fit, I got back out to my car and grab my computer. Since Rian already has furniture, I donated and sold all of mine, which made moving easier. Most of what I brought are books for the office, my electronics, and my clothes.

I pass Rian in the doorway on his way out and say, "Grab the blankets."

He smacks my ass. "Such a bossy Omega!"

In the past, the comment might have bothered me, but I'm no longer ashamed of my status. Instead, it sends warmth spreading through me, and I set my computer on my desk to rub my nape guard. The first of Rian's Marks hides beneath the metal plate at the back, placed there two weeks ago when I told him I had the all-clear to move.

Suddenly in a hurry to finish unloading the car, I leave my computer to hook up later and go out to grab my suitcases.

As I come back inside, Rian closes the linen closet

where he stashed my blankets and hurries forward to take the suitcases. "Here, I got this."

Suspicious about him not wanting me in the bedroom, I narrow my eyes at him. "Did you clear out half the closet for me?"

He tilts his hand from side to side in a so-so gesture. "But I'll make it work."

It came as a surprise to discover that Rian is a clothes hoarder. I guess, after growing up with limited space, he went a little wild once he moved into his own place.

When I first started coming on the weekends, he hadn't had room to even give me one drawer in the dresser. But we went through what he had and donated a lot of suits and dress shirts that he no longer needs in his new career.

Rian had settled on going into security, and he started working under Sean, who plans to scale back his shifts now that he's a married man and living at the foster home with Carrie. He wants to be more present in the lives of the Omegas they take in, and Rian is eager to fill the gap.

He'll be working a lot at the Walton building for now, which houses the OOP clinic and offers apartments for Omegas who have been in the program. His primary job will be to make sure that the Omegas who come to the clinic aren't harassed and to answer the calls from residents.

I grab the last box from my car and shut the trunk before heading inside.

Rian is nowhere in sight, so I drop the box in my office before heading toward our bedroom. "I already downsized my wardrobe, so you better…"

When I enter the room, I come to a stop. Candles fill every surface, with a large bouquet of roses sitting on the bedside table, and Rian kneels next to the dresser, a ring box in his hands.

My pulse quickens, and I grip the door for support. "What…?"

"I know it hasn't been that long since we got back together, but you never left my heart." Rian opens the box to display a thick gold band. "I asked you to move in as my boyfriend, but now I'm asking for you to live with me as my husband. Will you marry me?"

"When?" I blurt out.

"Um…" Rian blinks quickly at my answer. "Well, I hadn't thought that far yet…"

I fall to my knees in front of him and throw my arms around him. "I mean, yes. Yes, I'll marry you! I want to be with you for the rest of my life. I always have. Since the day we first met in high school, you've been the only one for me."

Rian hugs me back so tightly that I can't breathe. "I'm pretty sure we can apply for a license today, and get married in two weeks."

I pull back to stare at him. "That soon?"

"You asked when, and if I could, it would be today." He takes my hand and slips the gold band onto my ring finger. "The sooner we're married, the faster I can knock you up."

"What? No!" I scramble away from him. "At least let's enjoy the honeymoon!"

"That's what honeymoons are meant for!" He tackles me onto the bed and bites playfully at my nape guard. "Didn't I tell you I wanted a ton of kids?"

Laughing, I hook my ankles around his waist. "Two weeks, huh?"

"We've waited eight years to be together." He leans down to brush his lips over mine. "Don't you think that's long enough?"

"More than enough." I wrap my arms around his neck and pull him down. "I feel like I've been waiting my whole life to be yours."

Our love story took a few bad turns, and there were bumps in the road along the way, but the wait just made this moment all the sweeter.

At the perfect time in our lives, when we could commit ourselves fully, we had found our love at last.

. . .

The End.

∼

For more M/M omegaverse novellas, read the first in the Taken by His Alpha Series.

He's the Alpha real estate tycoon everyone wants. I'm just one of the Omegas who work in his club.
Claimed by the Boss

CLAIMED BY THE BOSS
Taken by His Alpha Book 1

He's the Alpha real estate tycoon everyone wants. I'm just one of the Omegas who work in his club.

There's no reason for Nolan Rockford to notice me, a masked stranger scraping the bottom of the barrel to survive. Left with a debt not my own, and one missed payment away from death, watching the powerful Alpha is the only light in my days. And the only fantasy that helps me through the nights.

Then a persistent customer goes too far, landing me in Nolan's lap, and my world turns upside down. Three nights. One Heat. Enough happiness to last a lifetime. At least, that's how it's supposed to go.

But Nolan has other ideas. He's used to getting what he wants, and my body is the next property he intends to own, whether or not I agree.

READ NOW

ABOUT THE AUTHOR

Sophie O'Dare is the alter ego of paranormal and sci-fi author Lyn Forester.

She loves writing stories about guys falling in love with each other and all the shenanigans that go along with romance!

www.SophieODare.com

REVIEWS

"This is an amazing coming of age story. There are authors that you know you can depend on to fill certain reading desires you may have. You know who to go to if you want a strong heroine or an action-packed story, sexy times or teenage angst. When you pick up a book by Lyn Forester you know that you are going to be transported into another world."

— Amazon Reviewer for *You to Me*

"Sota and Masa are simply adorable. I just want to wrap my arms around them and never let go. Sota's so clueless, but Masa's patience with him is perfect. I loved this book so much that I literally couldn't stop reading once I'd started. If not for work and sleep, I'd have been done last night. I can't wait to see what more Ms. Forester does in this universe, because I want to devour it all."

— Amazon Reviewer for *You to Me*

"Just Not You, the second book from the Tails x Horns series is a heartfelt, frustrating, tension-filled love story."

— Goodreads Reviewer for *Just Not You*

"WARNING: DON'T START BEFORE BED!!! I stayed up way to late to finish this book. I love how Lyn's characters are multi-dimensional and the world building is unique and complex. She doesn't disappoint with this next installment in the Tails x Horns series. If you love romance, give this book a try...even if you have never done MM romance before. It was absolutely stunning."

— Amazon Reviewer for *Just Not You*

Milton Keynes UK
Ingram Content Group UK Ltd.
UKHW031305220824
1354UKWH00022B/63